Hundreds upon hundreds of years ago, in a place called Flower Fruit Mountain, there was a remarkable little kingdom of monkeys. And by far the most remarkable thing about this kingdom was its king, who was known simply as Monkey King...

To the two loveliest boys
in the world, Melvin and
Darren, and the culture
that has nurtured me.
— D. C.

In memory of Shuching,
my beloved wife.
— W. M.

Text copyright © 2001, Debby Chen
Illustrations copyright © 2001, Wenhai Ma
Edited by: Frank Araujo and William Mersereau

Published in the United States of America by
Pan Asian Publications (USA) Inc.
29564 Union City Boulevard, Union City, CA 94587
Tel. (510) 475-1185   Fax (510) 475-1489

Published in Canada by
Pan Asian Publications Inc.
110 Silver Star Boulevard, Unit 109
Scarborough, Ontario M1V-5A2

ISBN 1-57227-068-3
Library of Congress Catalog Card Number: 00-107315

Cover and jacket design: Yudi Sewraj
Editorial and production assistance: Art & Publishing Consultants

Printed in Hong Kong by the South China Printing Co. (1988) Ltd.

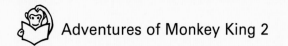
MONKEY KING

wreaks havoc in

HEAVEN

Retold by Debby Chen • Illustrated by Wenhai Ma

Pan Asian Publications

Monkey King had been born from a magic stone and had learned many powerful, mystical arts. His little monkey subjects loved him dearly – especially after he rescued them from some demons! He now decided that they had to learn to defend themselves. He trained a few thousand of them, and soon he had a very strong little army.

Monkey King was proud of his warriors, but something was still missing. "I need a royal weapon!" he declared. "It must show everyone what a great king I am!" An old monkey came forward and said that the Dragon King had a strange and powerful iron wand. Monkey King was delighted – he had always wanted to visit the old dragon's undersea palace.

Monkey King said some magic words and flew on a cloud to the sea. He skimmed across the waves and then plunged down, down to the Dragon King's palace. He marched up to the old king, saying, "I'm Monkey King. I've heard you have a powerful wand. Bring it to me!"

The Dragon King's eyes narrowed. "I've no such thing!" he hissed. Monkey King sneered, "Don't try to hide anything from me!" He pulled on the old dragon's whiskers. Wise Dragon King sensed right away that he could not match Monkey King's power in a battle, so he did not argue further. He swallowed hard and said, "All right, follow me…but I'm sure even *you* can't lift it!"

He led Monkey King into a dark forest of seaweed. There they found a glowing metal pillar. "This has been here for over a million years. Some say the gods used it when they built the starry night sky. It's fantastically heavy – no one has ever been able to lift it."

"Let *me* see about that!" Monkey exclaimed. He grabbed the rod and began pulling and twisting it. The ground crackled, sparks flew, and the ancient iron slipped free. On it was written,

Ruyi the golden rod which weighs 36,000 kilos

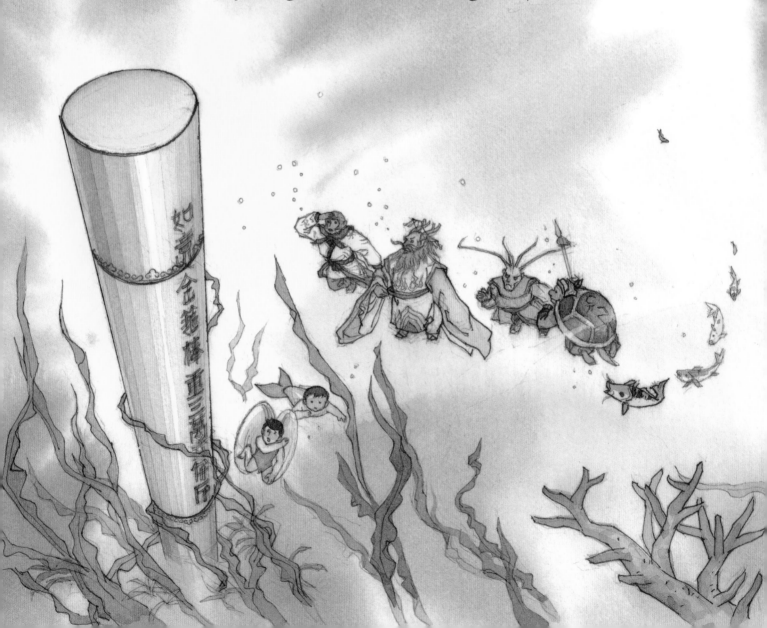

Monkey King frowned, "What does Ruyi mean?" Dragon King explained that Ruyi is the staff that grows or shrinks as its master wishes.

"Hooray!" cried Monkey King, "Now I can lead the Monkey Army!"

Dragon King was relieved to see Monkey King preparing to leave.
But before going, the naughty monkey helped himself to some
of the Dragon's finest clothes – including a red-gold cap made of
phoenix feathers.

Then, with a quick back flip, Monkey soared home. His little
monkey soldiers stared in awe as their king showed them the
glowing metal rod. "Shrink!" he shouted. Ruyi shrank to the
size of a toothpick. Then he shouted, "Now, GROW!" Ruyi
grew and grew. The ground shook as Monkey grew with it and
his laughter rang through the valleys. "Now we are invincible!"
he roared.

The Jade Emperor frowned, but then he smiled. "Monkey King of Flower Fruit Mountain," he said in a deep voice, "I appoint you my new Master of the Imperial Stables. You shall tend to the celestial horses." Now Monkey knew that very few people from Earth are ever promoted to a post in Heaven, so he felt very proud of himself.

Monkey worked hard at his new job, and the horses seemed to like him as their caretaker. But one day he heard two guards laughing at him. "What are you laughing at?" Monkey King demanded.

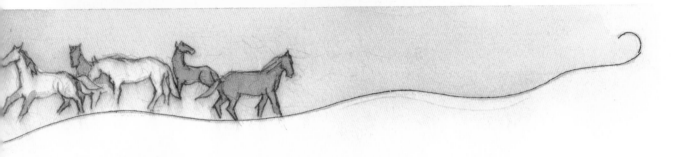

"On Earth, you bragged of your greatness," the guard snickered, "but here in Heaven, you clean dung from our stables! Ha! Ha!" Monkey King's eyes blazed, as he sensed the truth of the words. "Nobody makes a fool of me!" he said to himself. "I'll get that crafty Jade Emperor!" He threw open the stables and chased away the horses. And then with a double flip, he flew home. He ordered his monkeys to raise a banner on the top of Flower Fruit Mountain that read:

Monkey King the Sage Is Equal to Any in Heaven!

The Jade Emperor was genuinely angry with Monkey King –
first for turning his horses loose, and now for daring to declare
himself equal to any immortal in Heaven. The Emperor sent
his best warrior, the three-headed Prince Nazha, to defeat
Monkey King.

Monkey King stood his ground and fought Prince Nazha
brilliantly for two days and nights. Finally he split himself into
two. One monkey fought Nazha face to face while the other
jumped on him from behind.

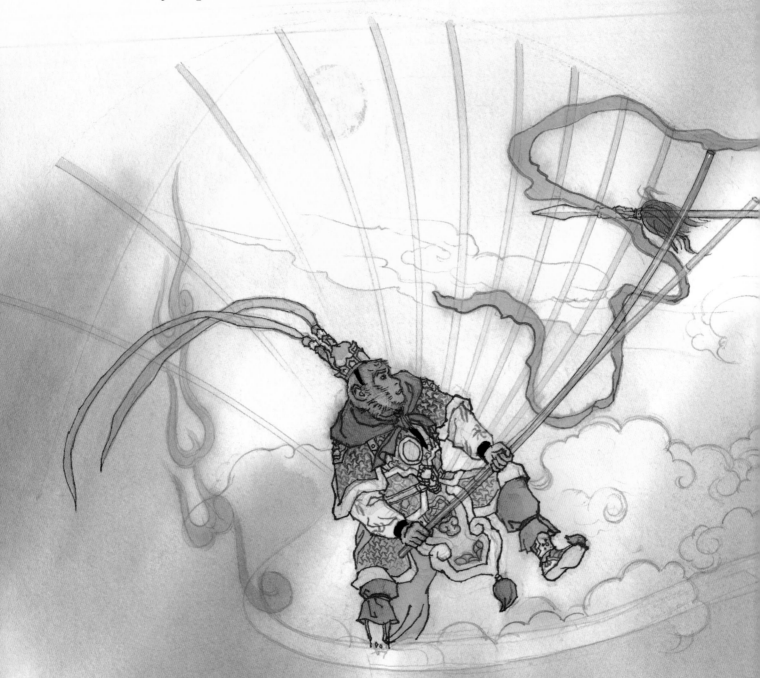

Prince Nazha then took a blow from Ruyi that could have flattened a mountain. More ashamed than hurt, Nazha fled back to Heaven.

Jade Emperor was hopping with anger when he learned of Prince Nazha's defeat. "That monkey must be destroyed! Call up my Heavenly Army!" But his trusted advisor, White-Gold Star, was worried. "Your Majesty, it would look bad if more of our fine warriors were humiliated by an earthly monkey. The best battles are those we don't fight. Let me talk to him. I'll make him the Guardian of the Sacred Orchards. It's an important but boring job, so it will teach him patience and responsibility."

Calming himself, the Jade Emperor agreed to his advisor's plan.
Sure enough, with some flattering words and promises of treats
and comforts, Monkey King happily accepted the job in the
fragrant celestial orchard.

Now, in one part of the orchard there grew sacred peach trees
whose juicy fruit ripened only once every thousand years.
Whoever ate one of these peaches became immortal. Monkey
King soon found some ripe peaches and, of course, he ate each
and every one. With a full tummy, he then shrank to the size of
a worm and took a nap on a leafy branch. Before long, seven
fairy maids appeared.

The maidens had been sent to pick the ripe peaches, but, seeing only green fruit, they burst into tears. Monkey King awoke with a start, shouting, "Hey! Who's crying?"

"Orchard Guardian, help us!" cried the eldest maiden. "Someone has taken the ripe peaches we were supposed to pick for Her Majesty's birthday party!" Monkey King jumped up. "A birthday party? Now why wasn't I invited?" The fairies then saw peach pits scattered nearby. But before they could cry out, Monkey King made a magic sign and the maids froze like statues of marble. "Now, let's find that party!" he said, setting off for the Heavenly Palace.

In the palace cookhouse, Monkey King smelled delicious buns baking. These special buns had magic spices that made whoever ate them impervious to both fire and pain. Monkey King plucked hairs from his head and changed them into mosquitoes that bit the bakers and made them fall asleep on the spot. The monkey gobbled up all the magic buns.

General Erlang flew down on his giant eagle to Flower Fruit
Mountain as the Heavenly Army fought the Monkey Army.
Erlang challenged Monkey King to single combat. Armed
with Ruyi, Monkey King clashed with Erlang. The
mountains, the seas, even the sun, moon, and stars all shook
with each dreadful blow. Erlang was the most powerful
opponent Monkey King had ever faced. The Monkey Army
soon retreated to Water Curtain Cave, their hideout behind
a waterfall. "Surrender now!" Erlang commanded Monkey
King. "The Sage Equal to Any in Heaven fears no one!"
Monkey King shouted back defiantly.

The monkey then changed into a sparrow and darted away from Erlang. But the great warrior became a hawk and chased after him swiftly. Monkey plunged into the river, becoming a fish, but Erlang turned into a heron and snatched him up in his long beak.

Monkey King then became a cobra snake and whipped Erlang with his tail before disappearing into the grass. The general regained his true form and stunned the cobra with a stone shot from his sling.

Now, for the very first time, Monkey King was injured and could fight no more. He crawled up into the mountains and quickly changed into a pagoda; his body became the walls, his mouth the door, his eyes the windows...and his tail stuck up like a flagpole. When Erlang found the strange building, he wasn't fooled by Monkey King. "Hah! A pagoda never has a flagpole!" He kicked in the door and smashed the windows with his sword, rattling Monkey King's head.

Taking his true shape again, Monkey King was now
caught. Luckily the magic buns he had eaten made
him feel no pain and the Emperor's potion quickly
healed his wounds. General Erlang tied Monkey up
in a rope of heavenly silk and hauled him before the
Jade Emperor. The Emperor's eyes smoldered. "You
have had two chances to prove yourself, but you
were too wild, mischievous, and selfish. Now, I'll
cook the magic out of you in my white-hot
cauldron!"

Monkey King just chattered and giggled as he was stuffed into the cauldron that was like a blasting furnace. After forty-nine days, the Jade Emperor finally opened the huge pot, expecting to see only ashes. But there was Monkey King, still jabbering away, still alive thanks to the sacred peaches, the potion, and magic buns. Only his eyes were stinging and red from the smoke, and this sent him jumping about in a rage. He took Ruyi from behind his ear and began smashing everything in Heaven.

The gods and goddesses fled in panic as Monkey shattered many beautiful temples and pagodas. The Jade Emperor was now very worried that the awful monkey couldn't be stopped. He sent an urgent message to the great Buddha, who came at once. Buddha smiled at Monkey King, "How can such a tiny earthly monkey cause so much mischief here in Heaven?" Monkey puffed out his chest and announced, "I'm Monkey King, the Heavenly Sage. I've beaten Jade Emperor. Now I will rule his palace."

Buddha's face was serene. "But here you have caused only confusion. It's true you have some great powers, but you're never satisfied with what you have. Do you really think you're wise enough to rule Heaven?" Then Buddha extended his hand. "If you can fly out of my right hand, the palace is yours. But if you can't, you'll be punished. Are we agreed?" Monkey King looked at Buddha's right hand – it was only about the size of a lotus leaf – so he shouted, "Agreed!"

Monkey King stepped onto Buddha's hand, then he soared up into the clouds. In a flash, he was eighty thousand miles away. He saw five rose-bronze marble pillars rising in the green mist. "Aha!" he thought to himself, "This must be the fence at the sky's end. I'll just leave my mark, then I'll go back to claim my prize." Using a brush made from his own hairs, he wrote on the middle pillar: *Monkey King was here!* Then, to be sure, he peed at the base of the pillar.

Monkey flew back to the Heavenly Palace. "I'm back from the end of the sky," he said. "Now give me the palace!" Buddha smiled, "Can you prove it?"

"Of course! I wrote my name at the end of the sky. Go see for yourself." Buddha held out his right hand. "Is this your handwriting?" Sure enough, on Buddha's middle finger were the characters Monkey had written. And there too was the smell of a monkey!

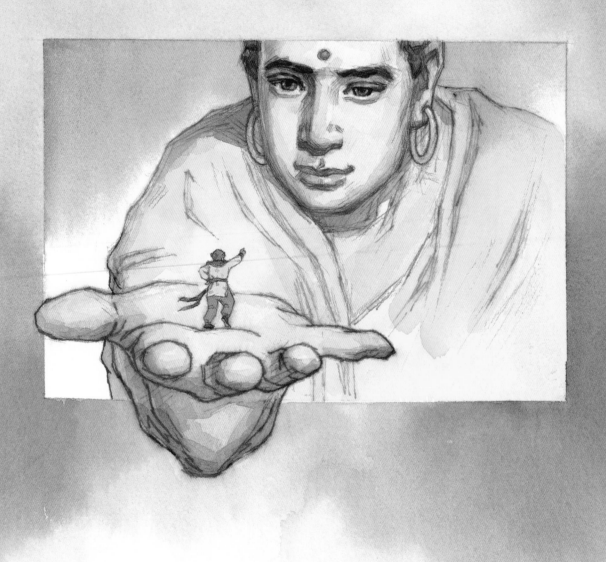

Monkey King tried to run away, but Buddha held him with his right hand. Monkey cried out, "Gentle-hearted Buddha, let me go! I'll be good, I'll change!" Buddha's voice rang like a golden bell, "You used your powers to bring chaos. You were given chances to be good, but you chose to remain wild. Now you must learn or be lost forever."

Buddha pushed Monkey King out of the gates of Heaven.
A reflection of Buddha's hand became a five-peaked
mountain that pinned Monkey King to the Earth. "You shall
stay there for five hundred years," echoed Buddha's voice.
"Five hundred years!" cried Monkey King. "How will I live?"

"Wet your lips with dew. Eat fruits that drop within your
reach. I have put a sign at the top of the mountain that tells
your story. One day, someone will take the sign down and
you will be free again." Monkey King groaned from his
cramped space, "Who will ever do that for me?"

"It is a person who is not yet born," said Buddha, his voice
fading into the mists of time.